JESSICA'S BOX

Peter Carnavas

First American Edition 2015
Kane Miller, A Division of EDC Publishing

Text and illustrations copyright © 2008 Peter Carnavas
First published in Australia by New Frontier Publishing
Translation rights arranged through Australian Licensing Corporation

For information contact:
Kane Miller, A Division of EDC Publishing
P.O. Box 470663
Tulsa, OK 74147-0663

www.kanemiller.com
www.edcpub.com
www.usbornebooksandmore.com

Library of Congress Control Number: 2014939758
Printed and bound in China
2 3 4 5 6 7 8 9 10
ISBN: 978-1-61067-347-1

For my family

PC

Jessica's mind was too
busy for sleep.

Her *thoughts* were already with
tomorrow.

And when tomorrow came,
everybody was excited.

"I remember my first day..."
started Grandpa.

"You'll have a great time,"
said Dad.

"You're going to make plenty
of friends," said Mom.

Plenty of friends, thought Jessica.
She was going to make sure of that.

At first, nobody noticed.

But by lunchtime, a crowd of curious children had gathered.
Jessica reached into the box.

"Ta-DAAA!"

Some children laughed.

Some tried not to.

Others just walked away.

"What's so good about a stuffed bear?"
a small boy asked.

"Lots of things," said Jessica.

"Lots of ... things."

Jessica told Mom all about her horrible lunchtime and how she didn't make any friends.

"You'll just have to try something else," said Mom.

So after thinking it over with Doris,
Jessica did try something else.

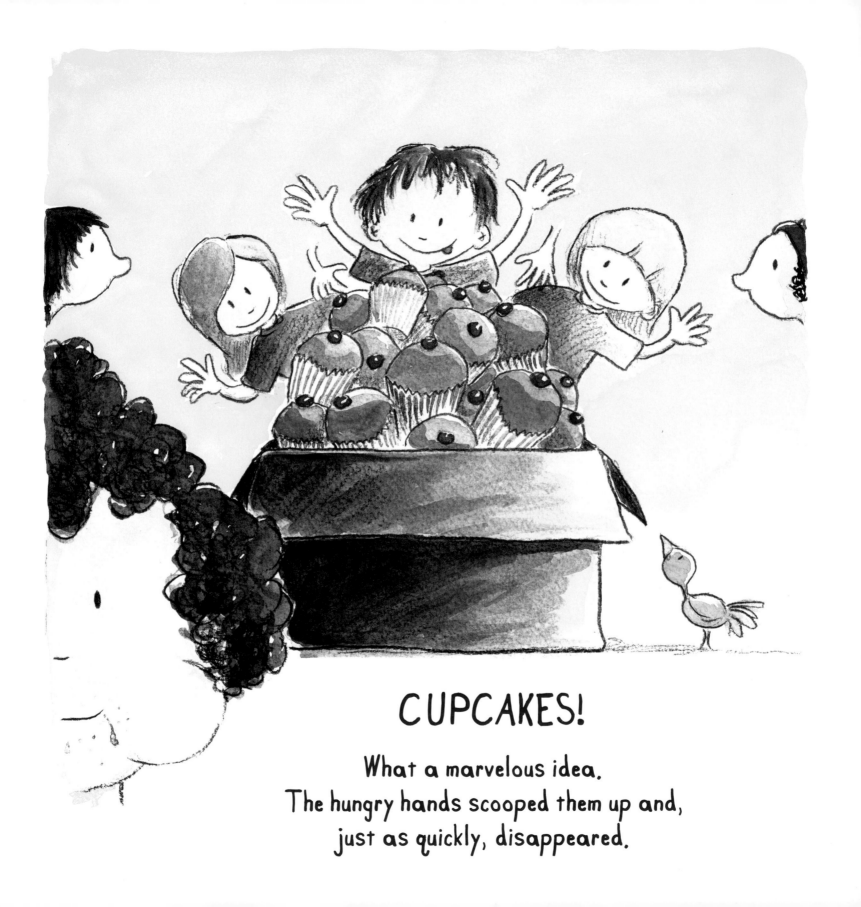

CUPCAKES!

What a marvelous idea.
The hungry hands scooped them up and,
just as quickly, disappeared.

Not even a *thank you?*

Jessica and Doris
thought even harder
this time.

And as Doris cleaned up the crumbs from the box,
a clever idea crept into Jessica's head.

"What's her name?"

"She's beautiful!"

"Can I have a pat?"

Everybody wanted to talk to Jessica.
It felt wonderful.

But it didn't last.
Within minutes the school
groundskeeper arrived.

"Can't bring dogs to school,"
he said, as he snatched Doris
and drove her home.

It was Dad's turn to talk to
Jessica that night.

They didn't say very much.

The following day, Jessica didn't take
anything in her box.

She just wanted
to disappear.

"Found you!"

Jessica peered out of the box.
"Now you have to find me," said the boy.
"Count to ten."

Jessica wondered for a moment.
Had she made a friend?
There was only one thing to do.

At home, the family was delighted to hear about Jessica's new friend.

Grandpa leaned in close and said, "You must have had something very special in your box today."

Jessica smiled and said, "I did."